The Not-So-Tiny Tales of

SimoN SeAHORSe

5

Into the Kelp Forest

By Cora Reef
Illustrated by Jake McDonald

LITTLE SIMON
New York   London   Toronto   Sydney   New Delhi

LITTLE SIMON
An imprint of Simon & Schuster Children's Publishing Division
1230 Avenue of the Americas, New York, New York 10020
First Little Simon paperback edition July 2022
Copyright © 2022 by Simon & Schuster, Inc.
Also available in a Little Simon hardcover edition.
All rights reserved, including the right of reproduction in whole or in part in any form. LITTLE SIMON is a registered trademark of Simon & Schuster, Inc., and associated colophon is a trademark of Simon & Schuster, Inc. For information about special discounts for bulk purchases, please contact Simon & Schuster Special Sales at 1-866-506-1949 or business@simonandschuster.com.
The Simon & Schuster Speakers Bureau can bring authors to your live event. For more information or to book an event contact the Simon & Schuster Speakers Bureau at 1-866-248-3049 or visit our website at www.simonspeakers.com.
Designed by Leslie Mechanic
The text of this book was set in Causten Round.
Manufactured in the United States of America 0522 MTN
10 9 8 7 6 5 4 3 2 1
Library of Congress Cataloging-in-Publication Data
Names: Reef, Cora, author. | McDonald, Jake, illustrator.
Title: Into the kelp forest / by Cora Reef ; illustrated by Jake McDonald.
Description: First Little Simon paperback edition. | New York : Little Simon, 2022. | Series: The not-so-tiny tales of Simon seahorse ; 5 | Audience: Ages 5-9. | Audience: Grades K-1. | Summary: After his friends tell him about the mysterious Kelp Monster, Simon decides to go into the kelp forest and catch the so-called monster. Identifiers: LCCN 2021053995 (print) | LCCN 2021053996 (ebook) | ISBN 9781665912136 (paperback) | ISBN 9781665912143 (hardcover) | ISBN 9781665912150 (ebook)
Subjects: CYAC: Sea horses–Fiction. | Marine animals–Fiction. | Monsters–Fiction. | LCGFT: Novels.
Classification: LCC PZ7.1.R4423 In 2022 (print) | LCC PZ7.1.R4423 (ebook) | DDC [Fic]–dc23
LC record available at https://lccn.loc.gov/2021053995
LC ebook record available at https://lccn.loc.gov/2021053996

Contents

The Story of
the Kelp Monster

"Race you to the top of the sandcastle!"
Simon Seahorse cried.

He was talking to his best friend,
Olive Octopus. The sandcastle on the
school playground was their favorite
place to hang out during recess.

But as Simon and Olive got ready to
race, something caught Simon's eye.

It was his eel friend, Nix. She was over by the seaweed swings with a small crowd of their classmates. She was talking in a loud voice and making grand gestures with her long tail.

"Hey, what's going on over there?"
Simon asked.

Olive glanced over. "Let's go see!"
she said.

When Simon and Olive swam closer, they realized that Nix was telling a story. The others were listening with wide eyes.

"And they say," Nix whispered, "that the Kelp Monster has been haunting the Kelp Forest ever since."

There was a long, spooky silence.

"Is that true?" a young parrotfish finally asked.

"Oh, yes," Lionel, Simon's clownfish classmate, jumped in. "I heard about the monster from my sister. She said its teeth are sharper than a red-bellied piranha's."

 "I heard it's bigger than a whale shark!" cried a lobster from another class. "And that it destroys the kelp in the Kelp Forest!"

Nix nodded. "My cousin said the fish that live there are so scared, some of them are talking about moving!"

"Those are just stories," Cam Crab cut in. "Have any of you actually *seen* the monster?"

Everyone was quiet again. It seemed that no one had.

"What about you, Simon?" Nix asked. "You must have some good stories about the Kelp Monster."

Everyone turned to look at Simon. Usually, he was ready to jump into a tale full of danger and excitement, but this was the first time he'd ever even *heard* of the Kelp Monster. For once he didn't have anything to say!

"I—I don't," Simon admitted. "Sorry."

The others looked disappointed as they went back to talking about the monster.

"Come on, Simon," Olive said. "Let's go to the sandcastle before the bell rings."

As they swam away, Simon thought about Nix's story. Was there really a monster living in the Kelp Forest?

"Hey Olive," he began. "What if—"

"Nope," she said, cutting him off.

"You don't even know what I'm going to say!" Simon protested.

"Oh yes I do," said Olive. "And I'm not going anywhere near that Kelp Monster."

Simon laughed. Olive knew him better than anyone. That was one reason they were best friends. Another was that when Simon's imagination ran wild, Olive was there

to pull him back to reality. And Simon was always there to encourage Olive to be a little more adventurous.

As Simon thought about adventure, he settled on something. He was going to find the Kelp Monster. He just had to convince Olive to go with him.

The Turtle Trolley

It was almost the end of the day and Simon was still trying to figure out how to get Olive to go with him to the Kelp Forest. Maybe if he promised he'd be patient while she examined coral specimens under her microscope? She was always asking him about that.

Or maybe if he wrote a special story just for her. Or maybe–

"Simon? Sea to Simon?" Simon's thoughts were interrupted by a voice. It belonged to Olive.

"Oh, sorry!" Simon said, a little embarrassed.

"I decided I want to go to the Kelp Forest with you," Olive told him.

Simon's mouth dropped open. "You do?"

"Well, I can't let you go by yourself, can I?" Olive said.

Simon smiled. Convincing Olive hadn't been so hard, after all!

"Besides," Olive went on, "I'm kind of curious. Not about the monster, but about the Kelp Forest."

"What's so interesting about the forest?" Simon asked as they swam away from Coral Grove Elementary.

"Well, did you know kelp can grow two feet taller in a single day?" said Olive. "And that it gets energy by absorbing sunlight?"

"Cool!" said Simon. He was glad Olive was there to tell him fun facts. But he was even gladder that he wouldn't have to go to the forest alone.

Suddenly, Simon came to a halt.

"Wait," he said. "I've never been to the Kelp Forest before. I don't know which current to take."

"I don't either," Olive said. Then her face lit up. "I know. We can take the turtle trolley! Come on!"

They hurried to the nearest trolley stop, which was just down the street from the school. As they scanned the trolley schedule, Cam scuttled by.

"Where are you two going in such a hurry?" Cam asked.

"To the Kelp Forest," Simon told him. "Want to come?"

Cam shook his head. "No thanks. I just got a fascinating new book about spider crabs. But have fun with the big, scary Kelp Monster," he said with a chuckle.

As Cam scurried away, Mr. Green, the turtle trolley, arrived.

"All aboard!" Mr. Green called. "Where are you headed today?"

"The Kelp Forest, please," said Simon.

Mr. Green honked his horn and pulled away from the trolley stop.

"Going to try to catch the monster, are you?" he called to Simon and Olive over the sound of the water rushing by.

Olive shook her head. "We're not catching *any* monsters! We're only going to look around. Right, Simon?"

"Right," Simon said. Then he smiled. "But if we *happen* to bump into a monster, it sure will make for a good story."

Mr. Green nodded, but he didn't smile back. "Just be careful, all right? You never know what's lurking in that forest."

As they whizzed through Coral Grove, Simon's stomach squeezed. Was searching—or *not* searching—for the Kelp Monster really such a good idea?

Into the
Kelp Forest

When the turtle trolley came to a stop, the sight of the Kelp Forest blew Simon's bubbles away. Towers of green kelp stretched out before him. The forest bustled with a rainbow of sea creatures.

"It's beautiful," Simon said. "And so bright!"

"I read that the Kelp Forest is closer to the surface than where we live," Olive said. "That's why there's so much light."

Simon's doubts melted away. He couldn't imagine what kind of "monster" could possibly live here!

"Let's go explore!" Simon cried. He thanked Mr. Green and swam toward the forest. Olive swam beside him, her notebook at the ready.

Among the kelp columns, they spotted tiny fish, barnacles, and starfish. While Olive furiously took notes, Simon admired the way the kelp swayed in the light.

"A purple sea urchin! Look!" said Olive, pointing to a spiky mound nearby. "I read that you often find those in places where there's a lot of kelp."

Simon was so amazed by the forest that he almost forgot about the Kelp Monster. Until something whooshed past him.

He whipped around, trying to see what it was. But there was nothing there.

"Simon, what's wrong?" Olive asked.

"I . . . I thought I saw something," he said.

Olive laughed. "Well, there *is* a lot to see around us."

"No, something big," he said. "Something like . . ."

"Like a *monster*?" Olive smiled. "Come on, Simon. We'll have time for stories later. Let's keep exploring!"

Simon sighed. Maybe he *had* just imagined it.

But after that, he had a hard time paying attention to all the amazing things around him. He was too busy keeping an eye out for the Kelp Monster. Just in case.

"Oops, it's getting late," Olive said, glancing at one of her watches. "We should head home for dinner."

Simon nodded. If there really was a monster, he didn't want to be in the forest after dark anyway.

"Race you back to the turtle trolley stop?" Simon asked.

"Ready, set, go!" Olive cried.

But as Olive took off, Simon froze. He had the sense that something was lurking in the shadows of the kelp nearby. And watching them.

"Simon!" Olive called out. "What are you doing? I thought we were racing."

Simon gulped. But when he glanced into the shadows again, there was nothing there.

"Uh . . . I'm coming!" Simon called. Then he hurried to catch up with Olive.

Otters vs. Urchins

"So, did you catch Kelp Monster yesterday?" Cam Crab asked the next morning at school.

At the word "monster," the other students in Ms. Tuttle's class fell quiet and turned toward Simon and Olive.

Olive shook her head. "Nope," she said. "But the Kelp Forest was *really* cool. Wasn't it, Simon?"

"What? Oh yes. It was great," said Simon.

He thought about telling everyone about the shadow he'd seen lurking in the kelp, and the thing that had whooshed by him. But he wasn't sure either had been real. So he didn't say anything else except: "We should go back and explore more of the forest soon."

"Okay, class!" said Ms. Tuttle, calling everyone to attention. "Since you're all talking about kelp forests already, you'll be happy to know that we'll be studying them today!"

Everyone hurried to their seats as Ms. Tuttle began the lesson. She told them about how kelp forests form in shallow water. "They're made up of different types of algae that grow

along the rocks," she said. "And they're home to all sorts of sea organisms!" She showed them pictures of many of the creatures Simon and Olive had seen in the forest.

"Any questions?" Ms. Tuttle asked when the lesson was over.

Cam raised a claw. "Kelp forests are also home to kelp crabs," he said.

"That's true. Thank you, Cam," Ms. Tuttle said with a smile. "Anyone else?"

"What about the Kelp Monster?" Nix said, raising her tail. "Do you think there really is one making a mess in our kelp forest and scaring the fish?"

"I've heard the stories," Ms. Tuttle said slowly. "But I can't say whether they're true. I *can* tell you that one real problem for kelp forests is purple sea urchins."

Simon frowned, remembering the one Olive had shown him yesterday. "But sea urchins are so small. How can they be a problem?" he asked.

"Purple sea urchins love kelp," Ms. Tuttle explained. "If there are too many of them in one place, they can eat all the kelp and destroy the forest."

Simon gasped. Kelp was Simon's favorite food too, but he'd never gulp down a whole forest! He thought of all the barnacles and tiny fish he'd seen yesterday. What would happen to them if the Kelp Forest disappeared?

"Luckily," Ms. Tuttle went on, "we have sea otters to help. They remove the sea urchins from the kelp forest and even eat them!"

Simon sat up. He'd never met a sea otter before, but he'd heard they loved to play games just like he did. He wondered if they liked stories too.

He couldn't imagine eating a sea urchin, though. Too spiky!

How to Catch
a Monster

"Want to come over to my house today?" Simon asked Olive after school, trying to act casual.

Olive's eyes narrowed. "What do you have planned now, Simon?" she asked suspiciously.

Simon smiled. "Nothing yet." But they needed to come up with a plan if they wanted to solve the mystery of the Kelp Monster.

"My mom doesn't need my help at the library today," Olive said. "So, sure, I'll come over."

Together they hopped in the current to Simon's house. When they arrived, Simon led Olive straight to his backyard. Since Simon had eleven

brothers and sisters, it was hard to find a quiet spot inside the house—and he needed somewhere quiet to tell Olive what he was thinking.

"Should we get a snack and hang out in the hammock?" Olive asked. It was what they usually did when they got together after school.

"Not today," Simon said. "We need to come up with a plan to catch the Kelp Monster."

"Wait, *catch* the monster?" Olive repeated.

"Yes!" Simon said. "Everyone keeps talking about catching it, don't they? Imagine how excited they'd be if we really did it."

But Olive didn't look excited about the idea. "I don't know about *trapping* something," she said.

"We wouldn't actually trap it," Simon assured her. "We'd just find it, talk to it, and let it go."

"Hmm, that *would* give us a chance to ask it why it keeps making a mess and spooking the fish," Olive said. It seemed like she was warming up to the idea. "But how are we going to find the monster? The Kelp Forest is huge."

"We can use something to lure it out. Something the monster can't resist," said Simon.

Olive's face lit up. "Like a good book?"

"That would definitely be the best way to trap *you*," Simon said, laughing. "I was thinking more like a catchy song. Or a really colorful picture."

"But we don't know what kinds of songs or pictures the monster likes," Olive pointed out.

"That's true," Simon said. This was harder than he'd imagined. "Maybe we *should* go hang out in the hammock."

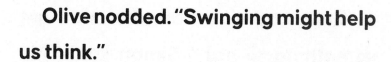

Olive nodded. "Swinging might help us think."

But after a long while in the hammock, they still didn't have any good ideas. And now Simon's stomach was rumbling for a snack.

"Let's take a break and get
something to eat," Simon said. "My
dad made kelp-chip cookies the other
day. I wonder if we have any left."

Simon and Olive looked at each
other. "Kelp-chip cookies!" they said
together.

"*Everyone* loves kelp-chip cookies, don't they?" Simon asked.

"Absolutely!" Olive said. "I bet not even monsters can resist them."

Simon jumped off the hammock. "Then let's get baking!" he said.

It's
Cookie Time!

In the kitchen, Simon and Olive started taking out ingredients for their kelp-chip cookies. A few of Simon's older brothers and sisters were doing homework at the table, so he and Olive tried to be quiet.

Simon's youngest sister, Lulu, swam over. "What are you doing?" she asked in a loud voice.

"Shh!" Simon said. "We're making kelp-chip cookies to lure the Kelp Monster."

He tried to keep his voice down, but his other siblings looked up from their homework. Their eyes were wide with surprise.

"Why are you doing *that*?" Lulu asked.

"We keep hearing stories about the Kelp Monster," Olive explained. "So we want to see if they're true."

"Can I come too?" Lulu asked.

"Are you sure you want to go with them, Lulu?" their oldest brother, Jet, asked. "I heard the Kelp Monster has yellow eyes and bumpy scales."

"And that it loves to gobble up sea creatures, especially the really small ones," said their sister Kya with a hint of a smile.

Lulu swallowed. "Actually, I think I'll stay here and play with my mermaid dolls instead," she said. Then she quickly swam out of the kitchen.

Simon chuckled as he grabbed a bowl and poured in some kelp flour.

"Are you following a recipe?" Olive asked him.

"A recipe? Of course not," said Simon. "My dad just uses a handful of kelp flour, a pinch of sea salt, a dash of squid ink, and—of course—lots of kelp chips."

Together, Simon and Olive mixed the ingredients together and spooned the batter onto a baking sheet. Finally, the cookies were ready to go in the oven.

"While those are baking," Olive said, "we should pack some snacks for ourselves."

"Good idea," said Simon. Otherwise the cookies might be gone before they got to the forest!

After they'd filled up a bag with snacks, the oven timer went off. "Cookies are done!" Simon said. The two friends waited a few minutes for the cookies to cool down. They smelled amazing.

"I hope they taste as delicious as they smell," Simon said. He popped one in his mouth and started to chew. And chew. And chew. "Wow, these are ... sticky."

"And salty," Olive added.

Simon frowned. "Maybe it was a *dash* of sea salt, not a pinch?"

Olive finally swallowed her bite of cookie. "I'm not sure that's the only problem," she said.

"What are we going to do?" Simon said with a groan. "We don't have time to make another batch today."

Olive thought for a moment. "Well, they *smell* delicious. Maybe that will be enough to lure the monster?"

"Good point!" Simon said.

They quickly dumped the cookies into a net bag and headed for the door.

"Let's go catch a monster!" said Simon.

Setting
the Trap

Since Simon and Olive had been to the Kelp Forest before, they knew which current to take this time. They hopped on and rode it away from Simon's house.

The delicious scent of the cookies was so strong that it got the attention of the other sea creatures they passed. Simon clutched the bag of cookies tightly with his tail. They were on a mission!

Finally, they reached their destination. The two friends hopped out of the current and swam toward the forest.

The kelp was so bright and beautiful, Simon still couldn't imagine how a monster could live there.

But as they swam into the kelp, they noticed a few rocks that had been knocked over on their sides. Simon remembered what he'd heard about the Kelp Monster tearing up the forest.

"The monster must have been here," Simon remarked. "Let's start our trail of cookies."

"Okay," said Olive, though her pink face was a bit paler than it had been.

Simon was a little nervous, too. But they were so close to finding the monster. They couldn't quit now!

Simon and Olive wove in and out
of the kelp, leaving cookie crumbs as
they swam. They made sure the trail
led back to the edge of the forest.
Then they hid behind a rock.

"Okay, the trap is set!" Simon said
as he held up one last cookie in his tail.
"Now what?" Olive asked.
Simon smiled. "Now we wait!"
And so they waited.

And waited.

And waited.

Simon didn't know catching a monster could be so boring!

Olive pulled out a book to pass the time, while Simon started counting fish swimming by. He almost made it to one hundred before he lost count.

"Want me to tell you about the time
I discovered a rare sea diamond?"
Simon finally asked.

Olive laughed and closed her book.
"Sure!"

Simon's mind swirled with ideas as he began. "It all happened one day when I was swimming near the old wishing well," he said. "Suddenly an eel slithered over to me. She said she'd heard about rare orange sea diamonds that grew around there, and she wanted my help to find them! So I–"

But Simon didn't get a chance to finish his story. Because suddenly a huge shadow passed over them. Simon was so startled that he dropped the cookie he was holding.

"W-w-what was that?" Olive whispered.

"I don't know," Simon whispered back.

They huddled together and looked up. But whatever had been there was gone.

Simon shivered. Maybe setting a trap wasn't the best idea. Maybe they should–

"BOO!" a voice boomed behind them.

"Ahh!" Simon and Olive screamed.

Pip

Simon whirled around. He expected to see a giant monster looming over them, ready to swallow them whole. Instead, he found a smiling sea otter.

"Hi there!" said the otter. He giggled as Olive and Simon stared at him in shock. "Wow, I sure gave you two a good scare. I'm Pip. Who are you?"

Simon was still too stunned to speak, but Olive said, "I'm Olive, and this is my friend Simon."

"What are you doing hiding behind a rock?" Pip asked. "Ooh! Are you playing Hide-and-Seek?"

Simon remembered how much sea otters loved to play games. "No," he said, finally finding his voice. "We're setting a trap for the Kelp Monster."

Pip's eyes widened. "The Kelp Monster?" he repeated.

"Oh yes," said Simon. "We heard that it's bigger than a whale shark and its teeth are sharper than a red-bellied piranha's!"

To Simon's surprise, Pip laughed. "Sorry. There's no monster around here."

"What do you mean?" Olive asked.

"I dive down here every day, and I've never seen a monster. It must just be a story," Pip said.

"There's no . . . monster?" Simon repeated. He let out a breath he didn't realize he was holding. He wasn't sure if he was disappointed or relieved.

"So much for our cookie trap," Olive said.

"Wait, you're the ones who left the cookies?" asked Pip.

Simon and Olive nodded.

"Thanks. I loved them!" said Pip.

"You did?" Simon asked. "They weren't a little too sticky?"

"And too salty?" Olive added.

"Oh, they tasted awful!" Pip said with another giggle. "But their stickiness made them perfect for pulling sea urchin spikes out of my teeth."

Simon and Olive looked at each other and laughed in surprise.

"I think I saw you two here the other day," Pip went on. "I was going to ask you to play, but you swam away."

Oh, Simon thought. *That must be who I saw lurking nearby.*

He was still pretty disappointed about not having found the monster, but he did enjoy meeting new sea creatures. "Well, we can play now if you want," Simon said.

"Great!" said Pip. "Let me just grab a few more purple sea urchins first."

Simon remembered what Ms. Tuttle had said about sea urchins eating all the kelp. Thankfully, sea otters like Pip kept them from taking over the forest.

Olive and Simon watched as Pip plucked a few purple sea urchins off the kelp. He pulled so hard that he accidentally yanked off a few strands of kelp, too. Then he tossed the urchins onto the seafloor, sending up a cloud of sand.

Just then, a school of tiny fish sped by. "Swim for your lives!" one of the fish cried. "It's the Kelp Monster!"

I Am the Kelp Monster

At the word "monster," Simon, Olive, and Pip all panicked.

"The Kelp Monster?!" Pip cried. "Where?!" He dove behind a rock and tried to bury himself in the sand.

Olive shrieked and curled up into a ball next to Simon.

Simon clung to Olive and looked around, trying to find the monster. But there was no one else nearby.

Then Simon noticed something. In Pip's rush to hide behind the rock, he'd accidentally tipped it over. Simon suddenly had a thought.

"Um, Pip?" Simon said carefully. "Do you think ... do you think that *you* might be the monster?"

Pip stopped digging. He blinked. "Me? What do you mean?"

"Well, we heard the Kelp Monster has been making a mess in the forest," Simon said. He pointed to the slanted rock, the bit of torn kelp, and the pile of purple sea urchins on the seafloor.

Olive's eyes widened. "That does make sense!" she said.

"But I'm not a monster!" Pip cried. "Why would anyone be scared of *me*?" Then he seemed to think about it. After a moment, he said, "I guess I don't really *talk* to the other creatures when I dive down here. And I *can* be a little clumsy when I'm in a rush."

Just then, Simon spotted a clownfish swimming past. When she saw Pip, she started to back away.

"No, wait!" Simon called, swimming after her.

"But there's a monster!" cried the clownfish.

"Pip isn't a monster," Simon said. "I promise!"

The clownfish stopped. "Are you sure? I saw him snatching up purple sea urchins earlier."

"Yes, he's just a sea otter!" Simon said.

"He's keeping the sea urchins from eating all the kelp," Olive added.

"Oh," the clownfish said. She turned to Pip. "I apologize for calling you a monster. We keep hearing stories about some big creature coming through and tearing up the forest. It's been making everyone nervous."

Pip looked embarrassed. "I'm sorry about that. I didn't mean to scare anyone or make a mess. I'll try to be more careful from now on."

"So you're really here to help us?" the clownfish asked, sounding relieved.

Pip shrugged. "I like diving down and searching for purple sea urchins. It's fun. Plus, I love the way they crunch!"

The clownfish looked a little worried again, so Simon added, "Without Pip's help, the sea urchins would destroy the whole Kelp Forest."

"In that case, I can't wait to tell the other fish the good news," she said. "We've been swimming around this whole time thinking there was a monster."

And with that, Simon, Olive, and Pip finally had a good laugh.

A Great Story, After All

Simon and Olive spent some time helping Pip clean up the rocks he'd tipped over and the purple urchins down below. Then the three of them played a few rounds of Hide-and-Seek together. Simon made sure to introduce Pip to everyone they passed.

That way the other sea creatures would know not to be scared of him anymore.

Finally, it was close to dinnertime, which meant Simon and Olive had to say goodbye to their new friend.

"Thanks for making sure everyone knows I'm not a monster," Pip said with a giggle.

"You're welcome," said Simon. "I'm glad we could help."

"Will you come back again soon to play?" Pip asked.

"Absolutely," Olive promised.

"And make sure you bring more of those kelp-chip cookies," Pip said. "Maybe you can make them even stickier next time?"

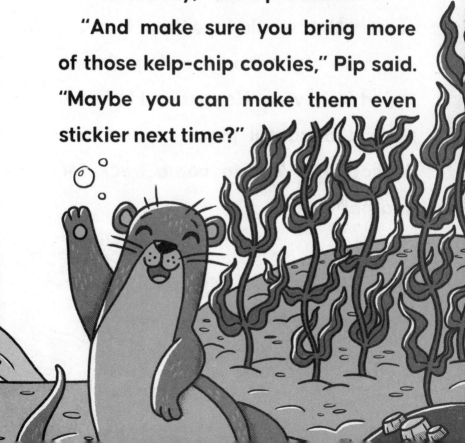

Simon laughed. "We can try!"

"But they might taste even worse," Olive warned.

Pip laughed too. Then he waved as Simon and Olive hopped back into the current that would take them home.

Simon sighed as the Kelp Forest faded from view. He was sad to leave such a beautiful place behind, but he couldn't wait to come back for another visit.

Beside him, Olive sighed too. "I have to admit," she said. "I'm pretty glad there's not an actual Kelp Monster."

"I am too. Even though catching a monster would have made for a good story," said Simon. "But it *was* kind of fun hearing everyone else telling stories for a change."

"I think I like yours better," said Olive. "They're not nearly as scary!"

Simon chuckled. "Thanks."

"Besides," Olive said, "your trap did help us 'catch' the Kelp Monster. Even if that monster turned out to be Pip. And meeting a sea otter who turns out to *not* be a kelp monster is still a pretty good story!"

Olive was right. Simon had a lot of great material to work for his next story. Which reminded him . . .

"Hey Olive, did I ever tell you about the time I tried to catch a glowworm?"

Olive smiled and shook her head. "Nope, but we have a whole current ride for you to tell me!"

And with that Simon began his next not-so-tiny tale.

SIMON'S STORY

Kenji was a small but *very* brave young seahorse. So when he heard about a monster that was haunting the Caves of Tritannia, he knew he needed to check it out. His best friend, an octopus named Alohi, was also very brave, and she decided to join him on this adventure.

The friends had never been anywhere as deep in the ocean as the caves, and the water was so cold that their scales and skin turned blue. But they kept going.

Finally, they made it to the caves and asked one of the deep-sea creatures about the monster. But the sea creature laughed. "We're *all* monsters down here!" she said. "All monsters?" asked Kenji. "Well then let's have a monster party!" And so they did. It was the biggest, loudest, most monstrous party the ocean had ever seen.

THE END

Here's a peek at Simon's next big adventure!

"Attention, class!" Ms. Tuttle said. "I have an exciting announcement."

Simon Seahorse looked up from his glitter sand painting. If Ms. Tuttle was interrupting art time, it meant she had something important to tell them.

An excerpt from *Shell We Dance?*

"The annual Coral Grove Elementary School Showcase is coming up," Ms. Tuttle went on. "Usually the whole school puts on a play together. But this year, each class will be doing a short performance!"

Simon cheered along with his classmates. Last year, he'd been a rock in the school play. Performing with his friends sounded like a lot more fun!

"Today you should decide as a group what type of performance you'd like to put on," Ms. Tuttle said. "And also choose a group leader."

An excerpt from *Shell We Dance?*

The bell rang for recess. Everyone cleaned up their art materials and then swam out of the classroom, chatting excitedly about the showcase.

"I can't wait to perform for the whole school!" Simon said to his best friend, Olive Octopus, as they headed down the reef to the playground.

"It *does* sound fun," Olive agreed.

"It sounds like a lot of work to me," said Cam Crab, scuttling past them.

Simon smiled at Olive. "*Sounds* like someone is feeling crabby today," he joked.

An excerpt from *Shell We Dance?*